Meerkat's Marathon

by Damian Harvey and Steve Brown

FRANKLIN WATTS
LONDON•SYDNEY

Franklin Watts
First Published in Great Britain in 2016
by the Watts Publishing Group

ISBN 978 1 4451 4773 4 (hbk)
ISBN 978 1 4451 4775 8 (pbk)
ISBN 978 1 4451 4774 1 (library ebook)

Series Editor: Melanie Palmer
Series Advisor: Catherine Glavina
Series Designer: Peter Scoulding

Printed in China

Franklin Watts
An imprint of
Hachette Children's Group
Part of The Watts Publishing Group
Carmelite House
50 Victoria Embankment
London EC4Y 0DZ

An Hachette UK company.
www.hachette.co.uk

www.franklinwatts.co.uk

What had he been thinking? Meerkat could never win a marathon!

A marathon is a very long race and meerkats are not very long at all.

As soon as they all set off, the other animals raced ahead.

MARATHON

7

But then Meerkat spotted Elephant, itching and scratching.

He didn't seem happy
at all.

9

Meerkat knew just what to do.

SCRATCH

SCRATCH

SCRATCH

"That's better!" sighed Elephant, and off he raced.

Elephant raced past
Chimpanzee who had
stopped for a snack.

Then he raced
past Iguana.

But then Meerkat spotted
Kangaroo, trapped by
a tree.

And she didn't look happy
at all.

Meerkat knew just
what to do.

"That's better!" sighed
Kangaroo, and off
she raced.

She bounced past Snake
who had stopped for
a snooze.

And she bounced along
past Bear.

But then Meerkat spotted
Lion, holding his foot.

And he didn't seem
happy at all.

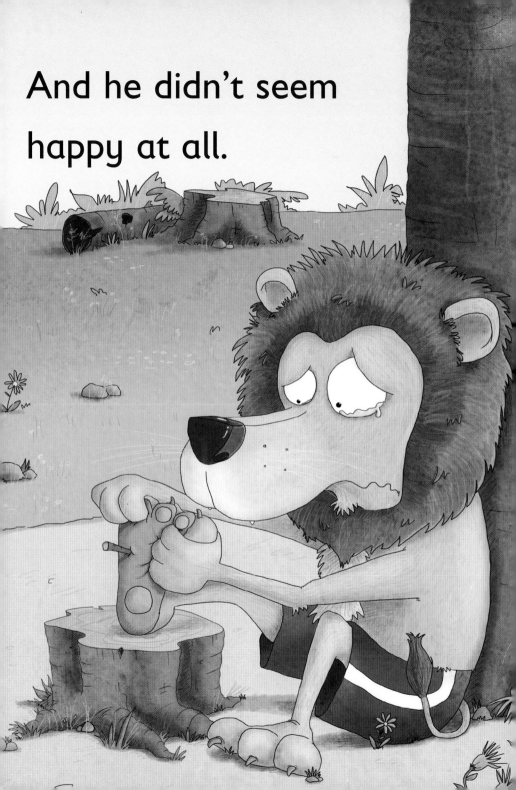

Meerkat knew just what to do.

POP

22

"That's better!" sighed
Lion, and off he raced.

He overtook Ostrich with his head in the sand.

Then raced past Zebra.

Soon there were no more runners ahead and the finish line was in sight.

As Lion crossed the line everyone cheered.

Meerkat had won
by a nose!

Puzzle 1

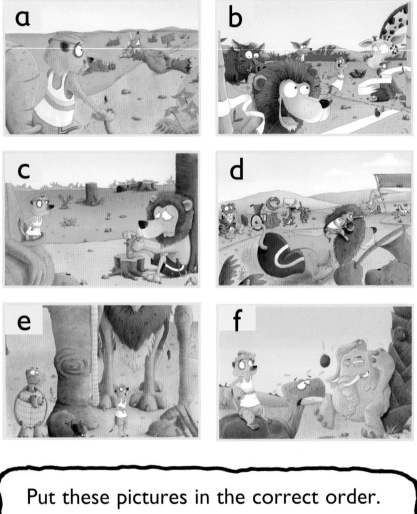

Put these pictures in the correct order.
Now tell the story in your own words.
How short can you make the story?

Puzzle 2

sad excited

nervous

hurt angry

upset

Choose the words which best describe the characters. Can you think of any more? Pretend to be one of the characters!

Answers

Puzzle 1

The correct order is:

1e, 2f, 3a, 4c, 5d, 6b

Puzzle 2

The correct words are excited, nervous.

The incorrect word is sad.

The correct words are hurt, upset.

The incorrect word is angry.

Look out for more stories:

Robbie's Robot
ISBN 978 1 4451 3950 0 (HB)

The Green Machines
ISBN 978 1 4451 3954 8 (HB)

The Cowboy Kid
ISBN 978 1 4451 3946 3 (HB)

Dani's Dinosaur
ISBN 978 1 4451 3942 5 (HB)

Gerald's Busy Day
ISBN 978 1 4451 3934 0 (HB)

Billy and the Wizard
ISBN 978 0 7496 7985 9

The Frog Prince and the Kitten
ISBN 978 1 4451 1620 4

Bill's Scary Backpack
ISBN 978 0 7496 9468 5

Bill's Silly Hat
ISBN 978 1 4451 1617 4

Little Joe's Boat Race
ISBN 978 0 7496 9467 8

Little Joe's Horse Race
ISBN 978 1 4451 1619 8

Felix, Puss in Boots
ISBN 978 1 4451 1621 1

The Animals' Football Cup
ISBN 978 0 7496 9477 7

The Animals' Football Camp
ISBN 978 1 4451 1616 7

The Animals' Football Final
ISBN 978 1 4451 3879 4

That Noise!
ISBN 978 0 7496 9479 1

Cheeky Monkey's Big Race
ISBN 978 1 4451 1618 1

For details of all our titles go to: www.franklinwatts.co.uk